GINGER GREEN

+Cousins =TOTAL CHAOS!

Ginger Green + Cousins = Total Chaos!
published in 2019 by
Hardie Grant Egmont
Ground Floor, Building 1, 658 Church Street
Richmond, Victoria 3121, Australia
www.hardiegrantegmont.com

 A catalogue record for this
book is available from the
National Library of Australia

Text copyright © 2019 Kim Kane
Illustrations copyright © 2019 Jon Davis
Series design copyright © 2019 Hardie Grant Egmont

Design by Stephanie Spartels
Internals typesetting by Kristy Lund-White

Printed in Australia by McPherson's Printing Group,
Maryborough, Victoria.

3 5 7 9 10 8 6 4 2

MIX
Paper from
responsible sources
FSC® C001695

The paper in this book is FSC® certified.
FSC® promotes environmentally responsible,
socially beneficial and economically viable
management of the world's forests.

GINGER GREEN

+Cousins
=TOTAL
=CHAOS!

hardie grant EGMONT

BY KIM KANE
& JON DAVIS

For my brother Jamie, who is VERY funny and was quick to point out that he does not actually have a book dedicated to him. And to his lovely family - Eva, Maxi and Penny (who is half-German but always nude).

- Kim

For Laura and Greta.

- Jon

CHAPTER 1

'My name is **GINGER!** Ginger Green.'

I am eight years old.

When I was in grade two, I was **really** into play dates. Now I am in grade three, I am still into play dates but I am also into **bigger kid things.**

I have my **very own** bank account.

I am learning to type with all of my fingers, **even my thumbs.**

TAP
TAP
TAPPITY
TAP

flip

I can make **heart-shaped pancakes,** and ...

I am now grown-up
enough to have a friend
sleep over at my house!

In fact, I am so
grown-up that my cousin
is coming to stay for

FOUR
WHOLE
NIGHTS.

That's right, my cousin Tess, who actually lives in

NEW YORK ≥ CITY ≤

is coming to stay with our family.

And she is not just staying for **one night**, she is staying for

FOUR WHOLE NIGHTS.

Baby me

Baby Tess

Tess is exactly the same age as me, only I am two weeks older. I know I am probably **smarter** and **more mature** than Tess on account of those two weeks, but I am too polite to mention it. Besides, Tess and I have only met once when we still wore nappies and we couldn't talk.

Tess is American so I know she will chew **gum** and I know she has her ears pierced. I also know Tess has probably been to a baseball game and eaten a hotdog. Those are the cool sorts of things American kids get to do.

Tess's little brother, Tom, is also coming to our **looooong sleepover.** Tom is the same age as my little sister, Penny, and may in fact be a bit **annoying** too. I think he is the reason Tess's family has not hopped on a plane since he was born. Uncle Jamo said he was mad to have another child (Tom) but he was not mad enough to hop on a plane with him. Uncle Jamo is my mum's brother and he is **VERY** FUNNY.

Tom and Tess have been staying at Grandma's house while their parents have a holiday. There is a **HINT** that Tom could be a bit annoying right there.

Aunt Eva ↓

Uncle → Jamo

Originally, Tom and Tess were not going to stay with us at all. They were going to stay with Grandma for the whole time but she found it all a **bit much**. And there is a second **HINT** already.

Tess

Tom

Tess and Tom only lasted **FIVE NIGHTS** with Grandma.

Lasted.

How many hints do you need?

At two o'clock the doorbell rings. Penny, Mum and I go to the door. Penny is wearing a **SPIDER-MAN** T-shirt that Grandma gave her. Penny is wearing the T-shirt with a **tutu**.

If you know my sister, this is a miracle. Not because Penny doesn't like to dress up, but because Penny doesn't usually get dressed **AT ALL**.

Mum opens the door and a tiny boy dressed in a cape and arm bands bolts past us and down the hall to the kitchen before Grandma and Tess have even stepped inside.

zoom!

'That must be Tom,' says Mum. 'I can see he's a bit of a livewire.'

Grandma looks at Mum. She says, 'He's certainly a livewire,' but her eyes actually say **@#$%¢*#¢%#$** which is too rude to type and certainly too rude to say.

'It's no secret why Mom and Dad needed a vacation,' says Tess, with a smile that looks a little bit like an apology. **I know that look.**

It is the **exact** look of a big sister who has a very embarrassing sibling.

eyeroll!

In my case, the sibling is my little sister, Penny, who is always nude. I like my cousin Tess already.

Penny looks down the hall after Tom.

'Don't even think about it,'

says Mum.

My mum is pretty smart and pretty tough.

That is what happens when you have a kid like Penny who is very quick to follow bad behavior.

If a kid is poorly behaved, Penny will ALWAYS follow them. My eighth birthday party was almost RUINED!

I am so excited to see Tess in real life.

She looks different from when we talk on the computer. She actually looks small next to Grandma, which is funny because Grandma is not tall at all. And in real life Tess looks even more American. Tess's hair is shiny. Her teeth are very white and she is wearing REALLY COOL SNEAKERS and a sparkly T-shirt.

Her ears are not pierced, though, which is a bit of a shame. The earrings I saw on the computer must have been stick-ons, just like mine.

Mum gives Tess a big cuddle.

'Isn't this a treat!'

she says.

'Five days with you both!'

Grandma, on the other hand,
does not look American.

Grandma looks
EXHAUSTED.

'I haven't seen you in ages, Ginger.

What about a cuddle!' says Grandma.

I throw my
arms around
Grandma's neck.

She smells like sunscreen and
lipstick, and the little peppermints
she likes to chew.

SHE SMELLS JUST LIKE GRANDMA.

Grandma lives about an hour away but we don't see her that often because she is **VERY BUSY**.

She plays golf

thwack!

and swims and power walks,

which means walking **really fast**,

and she seems to spend almost every night having dinner with friends or **going to the movies.**

crunch!

Not like my mum and dad.

They work

or **plonk on the couch** watching crime shows on TV.

snore!

Except for now. Mum has taken

a few days off work so we can have Tess and Tom to stay. I look at Tess and smile.
I am very excited to have my cousin here.

'Hey Ginger, where's your room?' asks Tess.

I CANNOT believe how STRONG Tess's accent is.

I cannot believe how American she sounds. She sounds just like a **cartoon kid**. Tess's accent is even stronger than it was on Mum's computer. Tess smiles and her teeth are so white they make me blink. And she really is chewing gum!

'I'll show you where we'll be sleeping!' I pick up Tess's bag. 'Is that **chewing gum**?'

'Sure. Wanna stick?'
She holds out the packet.

I take a piece, which I call a **piece** and Tess calls a **stick**. American chewing gum is so exotic. It tastes just like cinnamon.

My mum fills the kettle and says, 'Penny, you can show Tom your room too. Mum, sit down and I'll make you a cup of tea!'

Tess and I go to my room. Tess is going to sleep in my big sister Violet's bed. Violet is on horse-riding camp. Violet is a massive reader but she is not much of a horse rider. Mum thought it would be a good idea for Violet to do something **active** and to learn something **other than books.**

At first Violet said **NO WAY** but when she found out that not one but **TWO** younger cousins were coming to stay, she developed a sudden and deep interest in horse riding. She also took out the whole Pony Club series from the library.

Tess cannot believe the size of our bedroom.

'We live in an apartment,' she says.

'Your house is enormous!'

'It's not **THAT** big,' I say. 'You should see my fancy friend Isla's room. I still have to share with Violet.'

Tess nods. She shares a room with Tom.

I show Tess her bed.

I have put out

a soft toy,

a towel,

and a new pair of pyjamas. →

'Look!' I say.

I point at the little

fluffy koala holding a toothbrush.

I fish under my pillow and hold up my pyjamas.
We both have pyjamas with **glow-in-the-dark
stars** on them. Mum bought them as a special
treat. Penny and Tom have glow-in-the-dark planets
on theirs.

'How cool are these? We match!' I say.

'LIKE TWINS!'

'They are really neat,' says Tess.

I love the way Tess says **'neat'** instead of
'awesome'. I think I will say that from now on.
Even though I am actually not a neat person but a
bit of a messy person most of the time.

We go into the family room where Grandma and
Mum are having a cup of tea. They both like their
tea with a splash of milk. I wonder if Tess and I will
like tea with a splash of milk when we are older too.

Grandma is slumped down on the couch like she
could sleep for two hundred years.

'Thanks so much for
the PJs, Aunt Jess,'

says Tess.

Grandma gives Tess a hug. 'Tom is almost over his jet lag now, which is something,' says Grandma. Grandma suddenly unfolds and her back goes straight.

'Speaking of Tom, Tom is **VERY** quiet. Tom? Tom? Where are you?'

Grandma sounds worried.

'If one thing is for sure, we never get good news when Tom is quiet,' says Tess.

oh no!

'Where is Penny?' I ask. If one thing is for sure, we never get good news when Penny is quiet either.

Mum and Grandma both stand up. **Grandma LOOKS worried**. A few drops of tea spill onto the rug but Grandma doesn't even notice.

'Don't worry, Grandma,' I say. 'We have had a lot of practice with naughty friends. In fact, we are experts. When Maisy came over, she wrecked my birthday cake, stole Mum's car keys and danced on the roof in her undies. And when Olivia came over, she scribbled on the holy camel and unwrapped the Christmas presents.

A naughty cousin is going to be a walk in the park.'

Tess shakes her head. 'If that means "a piece of cake",
then nothing with my brother is a walk in the park.
You should see what he can actually do on a walk in
the park. Or with a piece of cake, for that matter.'

'**You're funny**,' I say.

Mum stands and starts walking down the hall.
'I'll check on the little ones. There's not much
they can get up to in ....

AHHHHHHHHHHH!'

CHAPTER 2

Tess and I arrive at the door to Penny's room at the exact same second. Penny's bed is **MESSY**. That is not the problem. Tom's bed is **MESSY**.

That is not the problem either. Kids like jumping on beds, even big kids like Tess and like me.

Penny's room has pale blue carpet. It is the colour of the sky and it is very **pretty**. **WELL, IT <u>WAS</u> VERY PRETTY.**

Tom and Penny have found Penny's wooden trains. This is not bad. Tom and Penny have found the textas. This is not bad either.

But Tom and Penny have not found the train tracks. The train tracks are right up high in a box on top of Penny's cupboard. Tom and Penny have **DRAWN** tracks in **BLACK TEXTA** all over the carpet.

THE TRACKS GO EVERYWHERE.

They go up over Tom's doona cover and Penny's doona cover. They go right along the bottom of the curtains where they touch the floor.

They go up the cupboard and across
the wall and over the carpet in
every direction.

all aboard!

Penny is pushing the train along

the tracks and Tom is drawing

even more

tracks just in front of her.

'KIDS!' says Mum.

'STOP. THAT.

RIGHT.

NOW.'

Penny stops straight away.
Penny **KNOWS** that when
Mum uses one-word sentences
she is **very cross**.

But Tom does not know.

He does not stop.

Tom drags his black texta further along the carpet,

making the tracks longer and longer, and then he

drags his texta up and over ...

the toes of
Mum's shoes.

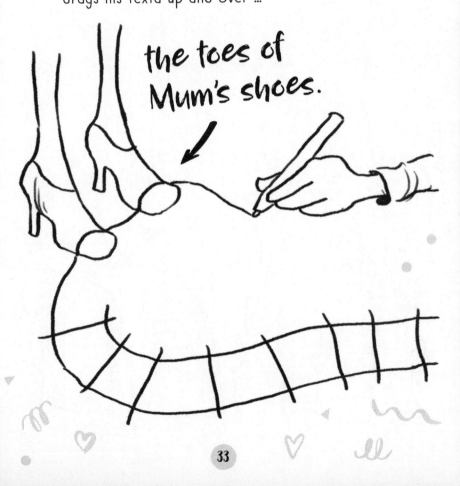

I stand in the doorway with my mouth open.

Tess stands in the doorway with **her** mouth open. Grandma stands just behind us, holding her handbag tight. She holds it up high in case Tom tries to draw across her handbag too.

I can't believe it.

Mum is **SO CROSS** she does not even shout.
She takes the texta from Tom. Then things go
from bad to worse. Mum holds up the texta. Only
it is not a texta at all. It is a permanent marker.
Permanent means *forever*.
Permanent marker never
comes off. It just fades
if you
are lucky.

'WHERE IS THE LID?'

Mum asks sharply. Her lips snip each word.

Mum gets down on her knees and looks straight at Tom.

'In this household, Tom, **we do not draw on the CARPET.**

In this household, Tom, **we do not draw on the CURTAINS.**

In this household, Tom, **we certainly do not draw on the WALLS or OTHER PEOPLE'S SHOES.**

You are a guest in our house and you follow **OUR RULES.'**

Mum is calm. Too calm. Her voice is calm and yet **VERY, VERY CROSS**. I have only heard Mum speak like that on the phone to work.

Mum turns to Penny. 'Penelope, Tom is our cousin but he is also our **guest**. Tom obviously does not know that we do not draw on the carpet.'

Or the curtains, or walls, or shoes, I think.

'Tom said he does it all the time at —' starts Penny.

Mum mows right over her words. 'But **YOU** know.'

Mum looks back at us.

'I am so sorry, Aunt Jess,' says Tess.

'I can't pretend Tom's normally well-behaved.
He's not. But boy has he been a whole new
kind of WILD since we've been here.'

'No need to apologise, Tess. As long as the kids
know they have done the **WRONG THING**.
But there is certainly no dessert tonight.'

'But we never get dessert, and
it's pink ice-cream!' shouts
Penny.

Mum looks at Penny and
Penny goes pink herself.

'Sorry,' says Tom.
And he looks **really sad**. He almost looks cute.
He hangs his head. He hangs his head so low that
his cap topples off and tumbles onto the floor.

'That's okay darling, I know it's hard having
your mum and dad away.'

Mum gives him a cuddle.

'Now, say bye to
Grandma. We are going
to have a fun few days.'
Mum's mouth winces
like she ate lemon.

Mum turns to me. 'Ginger and Tess, could you run a bath for Tom and Penny, please? I'll see Grandma out.'

'I should have left before the cup of tea,' says Grandma **under her breath**. Grandma kisses me goodbye. 'Thanks and good luck.'

GOOD LUCK?!!!

Tess and I take Penny and Tom into the bathroom and run the bath. When Penny takes off her tutu, I see the train tracks actually go **all along Penny's legs –** up the front of her thighs and down the back of her knees. They also go over the back of the tutu. I am glad Mum hasn't seen that yet.

It is the first time in **AGES** that Penny has kept her clothes on.

I look at my sister. 'Penny, I know that unlike normal people, you don't know much about clothes, but the **FIRST RULE** with clothes is that you **DON'T DRAW ON THEM. <u>EVER</u>.'**

'*I didn't,*' says Penny.

'Well you don't let other kids draw on them either,' says Tess. 'Honestly, Tom, you are going to end up in **JAIL** if you don't watch out.'

Tess takes off Tom's clothes.

She takes them off quite roughly.

'I will not,' says Tom. *He punches Tess.*

'Don't punch,' says Tess. She rubs her arm. It is already going a bit red.

'No violence in this house,' says Mum, walking in. Mum pulls off Penny's T-shirt and sighs. 'In the bath.'

Tom yawns a big, deep yawn.
He looks exhausted.

'Girls, would you mind keeping an eye on the kids while I start dinner?' says Mum.

'Sure,' says Tess.

'Sure,' I say in Tess's accent.

Tess laughs.

Tom and Penny hop right into the bath together. Because Tess and I are in grade three we will have a shower before dinner instead of a bath, and we will not have one together. Not because we have got puberty or anything yet but just because we are

a bit more grown-up.

Penny and Tom love the bath. We have a big bag of bath toys and they play with the boats and the sharks. They line up all the little guys along the edge.

Tess and I sit on the floor and talk. It's the first time since Tess arrived that we have had time to talk.

Little siblings can be tiring like that.

With Tom and Penny trapped in the bath, all we have to do is pick up the toys when they accidentally fall on the bathmat.

Tess tells me about her long **summer holiday**, which she calls a **vacation**, and all about Maine, which is where she usually goes with her mum and dad. In Maine they eat **lobster** on the jetty and **ice-cream sandwiches**, which are not sandwiches at all but biscuits with ice-cream between them in flavours like key lime pie.

Tess talks about how she is going to do musical theatre camp when she gets home because,

just like me, **Tess loves to dance.**

And Tess also loves to sing.

I tell Tess about the

SELF-PORTRAIT

I painted for Art with earrings and we both

agree we would look **much better**

with our ears pierced.

I tell Tess about a new ice-cream flavour I invented in my head called

Bottom of the Party Bag

which is a perfect mix of jelly lollies, chocolate buttons and bits.

Tess thinks *Bottom of the Party Bag* ice-cream sounds incredible. I have known Tess for a very long time but I have not known her all that well before now. Now I know I actually have the very best cousin in the world and she is exotic because she is **American**. Even if she does not have her ears pierced either.

MUM INTERRUPTS.

She calls,

'Dinner will be ready soon.'

We pull Tom and Penny out of the bath, wrap them in towels and send them off to get changed. Penny has been in the bath for an hour and the train tracks have still not come off her legs. They are like tattoos.

They could be there forever.

After our showers, Tess and I change into our **PJs**. They are **super cosy** and **exactly identical.** We look like cosy twins.

Penny and Tom are tucked up on the couch with Dad. They are in their **planet PJs.**

'The kids are tired,' says Dad, as if that explains **EVERYTHING**. As if that is an excuse for drawing all over Penny's bedroom and her tutu and punching Tess.

We eat **spaghetti bolognaise** for dinner.
Mum is really getting on top of her Italian meals
and it is pretty delicious. Tess and I pile on the tasty
cheese until Mum says,
'You have more cheese
there than spaghetti,'
which is just how
I like it and just
how Tess likes it too.

Penny and Tom are **SO MESSY**
when they eat I cannot even look at them.
Their faces and hands are stained orange
from the bolognaise.
They do not even
use their forks.

yuck!

Just as we are finishing dinner, the phone rings. Tess looks at the phone while Dad gets up to answer it.

'Jamo!' says Dad and he looks at Tess.

Tess's face splits into a giant grin.

'No, no. They're fine. Just finishing up dinner.'

'Daddy!' says Tom. And he jumps up from the table and tries to get the phone. Tom didn't use a napkin and he hasn't washed his hands.

DAD'S PANTS GET **ORANGE SPAGHETTI BOLOGNAISE STRIPES** DOWN ONE LEG.

'I'll pass you on,' says Dad.

Tom takes the phone and talks **on and on.** He tells Uncle Jamo about his glow-in-the-dark PJs and Penny's trains.

bad topic!

He tells Uncle Jamo about the spaghetti. Tess stands behind Tom just *waiting and* **waiting** for the phone.

When she finally gets on, Tom has been **TALKING FOR HOURS.**

'Dad,' says Tess, and she looks away. Mum points to the hall. Tess walks down the hall for some privacy.

ZZZZ!

While Tess is away talking, Tom's head becomes so heavy it falls into his spaghetti.

'Poor Tom is still jet-lagged,' says Dad.

'What's jet-lagged?' asks Penny.
'Does it mean your jet engines are slow?'

Dad laughs. 'Sort of. It means you've come from another time zone, like in another country, and you're *very* tired.'

Tom yawns again. Dad carries him off to bed. Penny is not far behind him.

'Let's hope for a better day tomorrow,' says Mum.

Tess comes back to the table. She presses her
fingers into the corners of her eyes.

Mum takes the phone. 'Are they having fun?'

'Yes,' says Tess, nodding.

Mum gives Tess
a quick hug.

I look at Tess pressing back her tears. I was having
so much fun with Tess I never stopped to think she
might not be having fun with us.

CHAPTER 3

My *looooooong* sleepover is off to a **BAD START**. One guest is in **trouble** and the other is in **tears**. I can't stop Tom drawing train tracks on the carpet, but I can at least try to make Tess feel better. **I <u>want</u> to make Tess feel better.** I want Tess to have fun with us. And I know just what will do the trick: **heart pancakes!** Tess needs something to look forward to. Looking forward to heart pancakes for breakfast always does the trick for me!

So, once Penny and Tom are asleep,
Tess and I get out everything
we need. Even raspberries.

yum!

The heart pancake batter
is **bright pink** and **smells delicious**.
We pour it into a pale green jug and put it in the
fridge. You may not know this, but pancake batter
tastes even better after a night in the fridge.

'I am so excited about our heart pancakes,' says Tess as we lie in bed. Her voice sounds happy.

'Me too,' I say. **'Heart pancakes are like a morning hug.'**

Tess is in her special PJs and I am in mine.

We are like twins. Glowing twins. I look over at Violet's bed and instead of seeing Violet trying to read, I can see Tess glowing right there like a STAR in my bedroom.

We are both tired, too tired to even talk,
and it is not long until we drift off.

I sleep long and deep until I wake in the
middle of the night to a noise. There is a light
on somewhere down the hall. And there is a

CRUNCH.

**I sit up
in bed.**

Even though the
stars on Tess's PJs have faded,
I can see that she is sitting up too.

'What's that?' whispers Tess. 'Is it a monster?'

'Too quiet for a monster,' I say. 'And I don't think monsters turn on lights. They like to operate in the dark.' But I have no idea what it is, and it is **SCARY**.

Maybe something got inside? I think.

When I went camping with my friend Lottie, something got into our tent and ate our midnight feast. Maybe something got into our kitchen.

'**DAAAAAAAD,**' I call quietly.

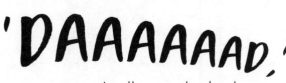 '**DAAAAAAAD,**'
I call out, a bit louder.

I hear Dad stumping down the stairs. 'What's up?' he croaks. I turn on my reading light. I am not feeling very brave but the light makes me feel braver.

'There's a noise,' I say.

Tess and I go out along the hall after Dad. We follow the light. We follow the noise.

CRUNCH
CRUNCH

We go past Penny's room.

Penny's room is dark.

CRUNCH
CRUNCH

The sound *IS* coming from the kitchen.

We go into the kitchen and ...

There is Tom sitting at the bench. There is Tom sitting at the bench with a bowl of **CORNFLAKES**.

The fridge is open. The fridge light is bright enough to light up the whole kitchen. The pale green jug sits on the fridge shelf just where we left it.

'TOM,' says Dad.
'WHAT ARE YOU DOING?' Dad rubs his eyes.

Tom looks up. He wipes his mouth with the sleeve of his pyjamas.

'Hi, Uncle Jon,'

he says.

'Tom, what are you doing?' asks Tess.

It is the middle of the night.

Tom is not in bed. Tom is not in bed, he is in the kitchen. Tom is in the kitchen sitting at the bench eating cornflakes by the light of the fridge.

Tess looks at the kitchen clock. 'Tom, it's three o'clock in the morning. **NOBODY** eats breakfast at three o'clock.'

'I was hungry,' says Tom.

Dad shakes his head and rubs the bit of skin between his eyebrows. He breathes out. 'Tom's tummy is still on American time,' says Dad.

'I can't tell the time,' says Tom.

Tess looks embarrassed. I squeeze Tess's hand. Tom stops chewing. **He yawns.**

'Bedtime, Tom,' says Dad. 'But tidy up first, please.'

Tom stands up. He carries his bowl over
to the dishwasher.

'Good boy,' says Dad.

Tom puts the cornflakes back in the cupboard.
As he is putting the milk back
in the fridge, **TOM SOMEHOW
TRIPS**. He drops the milk.
The lid is screwed on
tightly, so that is not so bad.
But as he falls ...

... **Tom knocks the green jug off the shelf in the fridge.**

The pale green jug with heart pancake batter in it.

'TOM!' I shout as the jug **SMASHES** on the floor.

'Everything okay?' calls Mum from upstairs.

'A-okay,' says Dad.

But everything is **NOT** a-okay. Nothing is a-okay. Bright pink batter pools near our feet.

'That was our breakfast. That was something to look forward to,' I say to Dad.

'I am so sorry, Uncle Jon.

He's honestly not usually this bad.'

Tess shakes her head.

I am finding this hard to believe. So far Tom has been in our house for not even a day. So far, he has **RUINED** Penny's carpet. He has **RUINED** Penny's tutu. He has **RUINED** Mum's shoes. He has **RUINED** Grandma. And he has ruined our special breakfast. Even if I were on the other side of the world, I would never do that. I'm not sure even my friend Maisy could manage all that either.

And we all know that Maisy is CRAZY.

TOM HAS **BRIGHT PINK BATTER** ON HIS TOES.

'It was an accident, Ginger,' says Dad.

'Some kids have more accidents than
others,' I say crossly.

Dad raises an eyebrow
at me as a warning.
'Girls, go back to bed.
I'll clean up.'

When we wake up in the morning,
Tom is already up and dressed.

He has built an
ENORMOUS
castle out of Duplo
using every
single
block we
have.

'Cool castle,'
I say to Tom.

'There's more pancake batter,' says Dad. 'Tom and I
made it. Blueberry this time.'

'Thank you!'

I give Dad a hug.

'Amazing what you can fit in when you get up at three o'clock in the morning,' says Dad.

'Didn't Tom go back to sleep?' asks Tess.

Dad shakes his head. 'Poor Tom is still jet-lagged.'

Tom is up and dressed. Dad is not. Dad is a **WRECK**.

He has a sip of coffee. 'I must get dressed for work.'

Tess and I are already dressed. We wanted to get dressed quickly so we could play outside. In the holidays I like to lounge around in my PJs, but Tess is more of a get-up-and-go type of person.

'Keep an eye on him,' Dad whispers to me as he heads upstairs. 'Tom is a good kid but if we want everybody to get through this visit

HE MUST NOT BE LEFT UNATTENDED AT ANY TIME.'

I nod. Tom is still building. I smile at Tess. We pull the pancake batter out of the fridge. This batter is **purple**. We heat up the frying pan. Soon blueberry heart pancakes are

SIZZLING

in the pan.

yum!

'Oooh, they smell delicious,' says Dad as he comes back into the kitchen. He is dressed for work. He gropes around on the bench for his lanyard. He grabs a Vita-Weat instead. He tucks the biscuit in his top pocket.

I take the
Vita-Weat out.
'This is your lanyard,'
I say to Dad, and
hand it to him.

Dad kisses me. 'Thank you. Let your mum sleep in. She was up until quite late writing reports.'

'Not as late as us,' I say.

Dad yawns, picks up his keys and heads out to his car.

'Do you want the first pancake?' I ask Tess.

'Yes please!' says Tess.
'What a perfect heart.'

Tess and I pour and flip pancakes until they are in a big heart-shaped pile. We pour big glasses of cold water.

I open the newspaper and find the COMICS.

We are just buttering our second pancakes when I hear Mum

SCREAM.

I look up.

Tom is not in the kitchen.

We were meant to keep an eye on him. We told Dad we would keep an eye on him, but we forgot ...

CHAPTER 4

Tess and I RUN down the hall.

We get to Penny's room. Mum is there.

'Not another permanent marker?' I ask.

Mum shakes
her head.

Tom's bed is messy. That is
not enough to make Mum yell.

The curtains are still shut. That is not enough
to make Mum yell either.

The pyjamas Mum bought, the glow-in-the-dark planet ones, **are all cut up**. Tom and Penny have cut out all the planets. They have not cut very well.

They have also cut up **OUR** glow-in-the-dark PJs.

Tom is holding a pair of scissors.

He is cutting out a star.

oh no!

I snatch the pyjamas from Tom. Now I yell.

'We have only worn them once.

THAT IS NOT FAIR.

Tess and I were twins.

We were glowing

twins and now

EVERYTHING IS RUINED.'

The pyjamas really are ruined.

They are not really pyjamas anymore. They are mainly holes. Like Swiss cheese.

'Scissors,' says Mum in another one-word sentence.

Tom and Penny hand their scissors to Mum.

I AM STILL ANGRY.

I am so angry I am red.

'That is not good enough, Penny,'

I say. '**YOU** might not wear

clothes, **YOU** might choose not to

wear clothes, but I do. **I LOVE them**.'

I burst into tears. I know I am probably a bit old to

cry, but I am tired and sad. I loved my pyjamas.

'You are a monster,' I shout at Tom.

'And you are too,' I scream at Penny. 'Mini monsters,

but monsters. Both of you.'

Penny bursts into tears.

'Sorry,' whispers Tom.

His bottom lip trembles.

'What were you thinking?' asks Mum.
She pushes her glasses up her nose. It is so early
Mum does not even have her contact lenses in.

'I have **stars** and **moons** on my roof at home,' says Tom.

'They glow. I wanted moons and stars on Penny's
roof so when I wake up in the middle of the night,
it would feel like home. Then I wouldn't need
cornflakes.' **Tom starts to cry too.**

I feel a bit bad. I feel a bit bad Tom is missing home so much that he is trying to make our home look like his home.

Mum shakes her head. 'Tom and Penny, you stay here with me and help tidy up. Then you can have ten minutes of quiet time. Tess and Ginger, head back to the kitchen.'

Tess and I walk down the hall. 'Tom is homesick,' I say to Tess.

'I am too,' says Tess. Her eyes get wet and she starts to cry.

'Have you ever been homesick?' she asks.

I nod and put my arm around Tess as we walk into the kitchen.

'When I went on a sleepover at Lottie's house I got very homesick,' I say. 'I just wanted to go home, and that sleepover was only for one night and in the same country, even if we did sleep in a tent.'

'You slept in a tent?' asks Tess. 'Cool.'

'But Lottie's mum dressed up as a banana in the middle of the night, which was scary,' I say.

Tess laughs.

It wasn't that funny at the time.

Then Tess sniffs. 'Sorry,' she says. 'You are all so kind and funny, but I guess I just miss Mom and Dad and school and New York and cupcakes.'

I've never tasted American cupcakes before, but I do understand that although my cousins are cool and kind and naughty, they are still a long way from their parents and a long, long way from home.

Tom and Penny walk back into the kitchen. I frown.

I am still **ANGRY** about
the pyjamas. I give Tess a hug.

And then
suddenly I smile.

'I have
an idea,'
I say.

CHAPTER 5

Tess and Tom are **HOMESICK** but they are homesick in different ways. Tess cries when she is homesick but Tom is naughty. I'm not sure that there is a total cure for homesickness but there is definitely a Band-aid.

I fill Tess in on my plans. She **LOVES** them.

First we get a **piece of string** and four little **paper bags**. We hang up the string like a clothesline in the kitchen. We decorate the bags.

On the last one I write

'Mommy and Daddy ARRIVE!'

I even remember to spell 'Mommy' the **American** way!

I get out four **wooden pegs** and stamp numbers on them with a stamp kit and ink.

Then I put two tiny treats in each bag — one for Tess and one for Tom. I mainly put in stickers and squishies that smell like lollies, but I also put two mini glitter pens in the last bag.

Once the bags are decorated and filled, we peg them on the string.

'What is it?' asks Tom. 'I love the pegs.'

'It's a COUNTDOWN CALENDAR,' I say.

'You know how we have an **advent calendar** that counts down the days until Christmas? Well, this one counts down the days until we see Mommy and Daddy again,' explains Tess. 'Ginger thought of it!'

'So I get to open a bag today?' asks Tom.

'You do!' I say.
'IF YOU ARE GOOD.'

'Neat!' says Tom. 'I'll be good.'

'I just wish I had thought of that yesterday!'
says Mum.

'Not as much as Grandma does!' says Tess.

Next, Tess and I go through all the selfies on the computer and find pictures of Uncle Jamo and Aunt Eva.

We print them out really big and stick them on paper plates.

We stick a coathanger to the back of each plate-face and dress the coathangers in clothes from Mum and Dad's wardrobe.

Then we stuff the clothes with paper. We make a **SCARECROW UNCLE** and a **SCARECROW AUNT!**

We hang them from a tree in the garden and Tess and Tom take turns hugging them. I work the arms to make them talk and hug back like **BIG PUPPETS**.

I even use the special **American accent** I've been practising.

'**Geez you've grown!**'

'**Don't forget your manners!**'

'Hey Ginger, have you thought about selling **Bottom of the Party Bag** ice-cream to help buy a plane ticket to New York?'

'Don't forget to hang up the bathmat and eat your broccoli.'

When I say that bit, Tom stops and smiles.

'I don't miss Mommy or Daddy when they ask me to do chores,' he says. 'Let's go and play, Penny!'

Penny and Tom run off to play.

'Selling Bottom of the Party Bag ice-cream is a cool idea!' says Tess. 'We really could save up for a ticket for you to come to New York.'

imagine!

Bottom of the Party Bag

ice-cream is a **cool idea** but I've got an even **BETTER** idea. Tess and I go back into the kitchen and make cupcakes.

Once the cupcakes have cooled, we carve holes into them and put in some cut-up bits of lollies so when you bite into them you get a surprise.

Like a piñata.

double yum!

'Bottom of the Party Bag cupcakes?' asks Tess.
'You got it!'

Next, we make buttercream icing.
We put the icing in a bag and pipe it onto the
cupcakes. We cover them in sprinkles.

'Incredible,'

says Tess.

We take the cupcakes outside.

'They are too beautiful to eat,' says Tess.

'Not that beautiful,' I say. I take a bite.

I offer them to my puppet aunt and uncle.

I can see they want a bite but

they are making

healthy choices.

Tess and I are happily making
unhealthy choices. We have
a cupcake each on the grass.

We have sprinkles on our lips. We wash them
off with big glasses of water. We stare up through
the leaves of the tree. 'Does the cupcake bit taste
like home?' I ask.

Tess frowns.

'If you close your eyes are you right
    back in New York City?'

'No.'

'Oh.'

I feel disappointed.
I tried really hard.

Tess grins. 'I've had cupcakes in New York but I have never had **Bottom of the Party Bag** cupcakes! They are totally original.'

I smile. 'Do you like them?'

'I **LOVE** them. I love _all_ of this.

I do miss home but at home, we don't have a yard. We don't even have a balcony. Also, it is freezing outside but too hot inside. Here I get to be on vacation and play in shorts and a T-shirt and lie on the grass in your very own yard and eat cupcakes.

That's pretty neat.'

* ★ ✱ ★ ✱ ★ *

Three days later,
Tess and Tom unpeg
the last bag from the

COUNTDOWN
CALENDAR.

There is a jar
on our kitchen
counter labelled
'New York Fund'
and it is full
of coins. Who knew my

Bottom of the Party Bag cupcakes
would be such a hit? The neighbours
bought hundreds!

finally!

Uncle Jamo and Aunt Eva arrive to collect Tess and Tom at lunchtime. Aunt Eva and Uncle Jamo are **tanned** and **relaxed**. Uncle Jamo is wearing a shell necklace.

Uncle Jamo looks at the coin jar. 'Well, that is something to get excited about, isn't it, Tess?!'

TESS AND I NOD **WILDLY**.

'I'm hoping to retire soon,' says Mum, nodding at my jar.

Uncle Jamo smiles. 'How's Mum?'

He is talking about Grandma.

'Looking forward to seeing us all for the party tomorrow,' says Mum.

'Did you have a good holiday?' I ask.

'We had the best holiday **EVER**,' yells Tom.

'Ginger wasn't actually asking you, Tom,' says Tess, and laughs. 'But we did, *we actually did!*'

AND TESS IS RIGHT.

When a sleepover is a super long sleepover, like four nights, your friend can get **HOMESICK** — even if your friend is both your friend AND your cousin.

But that's okay.

Because even with a bit of homesickness,
everyone can still have a **great time**.
It just takes a few ideas.

And Tess and I are
ALWAYS the kids for that.

THE END

HOW TO FIX Home-Sickness

I did **HEAPS** of fun activities when my American cousins came to stay.

You can do them too! You could do them with your own friends or even your cousins.

Don't worry if your cousins are not from an exciting place like New York City, I bet they will like these activities anyway.

COUNTDOWN
Calendars

Countdown calendars are fantastic and really you could use them for **anything**. Since I made one for Tess and Tom, we have used them at home to count down the number of days until Mum comes back from a conference, to count down the number of days until BOOK WEEK and to count down to the first day of school after the loooooooooooong summer holidays.

You will need something to put treats into **(like paper bags),**

ribbon or **string** to hang them from,

and **pegs.**

Sometimes I use paper bags for the treats and sometimes I use **envelopes**. There are so many ways to decorate them.

You could just use **pencils** and **textas** (**NOT** permanent markers!) and **stickers**, or you could even make your own stamps from fruit. **Yes, fruit.** It is a healthy choice. Ask an adult to slice an apple in half. Dip the cut half in paint (acrylic paint works best) and use it as a stamp. Just don't eat the fruit afterwards because it will be covered in paint, which is never a healthy choice!

Once they are dry, I fill my bags with little things — lollies, squishies, glitter pens. The one I made for Mum's long weekend countdown calendar had different types of seeds in every bag and finished with a tulip bulb. **She LOVED it!**

FLOWER SEEDS

I like to decorate the ← pegs too.

I use my NUMBER STAMPS on the pegs but you could even draw numbers on the pegs (or on the bags themselves). Remember to keep the numbered pegs as they can definitely be used again!

Next you need to make a line to hang them on, a bit like a clothesline. Sometimes I use **string** and sometimes **pretty ribbon**. Once the bags or the envelopes are filled, peg them up on the line.

You are ready to count down!

BOTTOM OF THE PARTY BAG
Cupcakes

This is my **favourite** cupcake batter recipe but if you already have your own, use that instead! (Or you could use a packet mix!)

3/4 cup of milk

1/2 cup of sugar

125g of butter, cut into cubes

2 eggs, beaten

1 teaspoon of vanilla essence

1 1/2 cups of self-raising flour, sifted

INGREDIENTS FOR THE BUTTERCREAM

3 cups of icing sugar

250g of butter, cut into cubes

1 tablespoon of milk

1 tablespoon of lemon zest

food colouring (if you like!)

FOR THE BOTTOM OF THE PARTY BAG MIX:

Ask an adult to help you cut up a mixture of lollies.

I am talking **licorice allsorts, snakes, M&Ms** all cut up into bits.

(If you are not allowed to use a sharp knife, you can cut up lolly snakes with scissors. Just don't use the material scissors. I did that and Dad got really cross!).

Add some **sprinkles** and **little silver balls** to the mix to make it look really pretty!

TO MAKE THE CUPCAKES:

Turn oven on to 180°C so it heats up. Line a cupcake tin with patty pans.

I use those pretty silver ones!

STEP 1

Mix the sugar and butter with an electric mixer.

STEP 2

Add the beaten eggs, a little at a time, and mix well.

STEP 3

Add the milk and vanilla essence and mix again.

STEP 4

Add the sifted **self-raising flour** last and stir it through by hand (use a wooden spoon). The more you stir, the flatter the cupcakes will be, so I don't stir too much.

STEP 5

Spoon some **batter** into each patty pan. You want each pan to be about two-thirds full.

yum!

Ask an adult to help you put the tin into the oven.

Cook until ⇒ **golden** ⇐
on top. This usually takes
about 15 to 20 minutes.

When you think
they are ready,
ask a grown-up to
remove the tin from
the oven.

Stick a **toothpick** in a
cupcake to make sure they have
cooked all the way through.
If the toothpick comes out **DRY**
or **WITH CAKE CRUMBS**
ON IT, they are cooked. ➜

⬅ If the toothpick comes
out **WET**, they're not cooked yet.

Leave them to sit in the cupcake
tin for five minutes.

Then take them out of the tin and place them on a cooling rack. Let them cool before you start the next step!

TO MAKE THE BUTTERCREAM:

STEP 1 Use an electric mixer to whizz up all the buttercream ingredients together.

STEP 2 Whip for at least five minutes so buttercream is light and fluffy. Sometimes I whizz it for ten minutes. Add the milk and vanilla essence and mix again.

You can add a few drops of any colour food colouring you like but I quite like the plain buttercream. Besides, Mum says food colouring makes us **CRAZY**. And Penny's already **CRAZY** enough.

TO ASSEMBLE THE CUPCAKES:

STEP 1   Once the cakes are properly cool, get a sharp knife and cut out the top of every cupcake.

STEP 2   **You will need a grown-up to help you.**

Cut out a triangle-shaped wedge of cake like this.

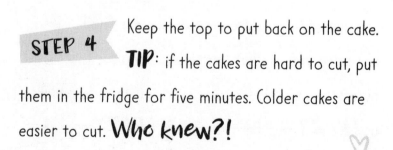

STEP 3   Slice off the bottom of the wedge.

STEP 4   Keep the top to put back on the cake.
TIP: if the cakes are hard to cut, put them in the fridge for five minutes. Colder cakes are easier to cut. **Who knew?!**

Fill each hole with **Bottom of the Party Bag** mix.

Place the top back on each cupcake to seal it and then ice them all over with buttercream. Sometimes I place a bit of extra buttercream on the cupcake top to keep it in place.

Serve and watch your friend's surprise when they bite into the cupcake!

You can also mix **Bottom of the Party Bag** through ice-cream. Let vanilla ice-cream melt a bit, mix it through the soft ice-cream and then refreeze. Trust me, it is incredible. I cannot work out why it has not taken off. Hopefully, however, together with the cupcakes it will help **ME** take off!

FAMILY Puppets

I love these because they are **so silly**.

Find a **SELFIE** of every member of your family.
Print them on the computer at A4 size.

Carefully cut out the heads.

Place the heads on a
  paper plate
    and glue
  them in place.

Then tape the paper plate head to a coathanger.

Put a shirt on the coathanger. Use something your mum and dad really wear to make it look more realistic.

You can even thread your arms through the sleeves if you want moving arms, or stuff them with paper like Tess and I did.

Now you can pretend to be your parents.

Act out your family or your school friends.

BODY
Chalk

Go outside. Find some concrete, like the footpath or your driveway. Draw around the outside of your body with chalk.

Play 'fill in the outline'. Draw something you would really like to wear – a **SPACE SUIT** with

a NASA sign or a **clown outfit** or a
Royal Dress you could wear to a ball.

arrr!

argh!

Otherwise, swap with your
friend or sibling and fill in each
other's chalk outline.
Draw clothes. Draw
costumes. Draw a bellybutton
and just walk away if
you have swapped
with Penny!

Foxigami

I love origami. I think it's incredible that you can fold paper to make almost anything at all!

TO MAKE ME:

You will need a square piece of paper. Brown or orange paper is the most **foxy!**

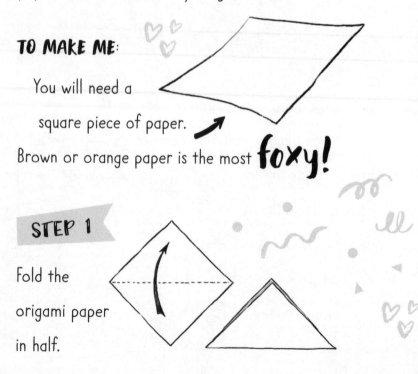

STEP 1

Fold the origami paper in half.

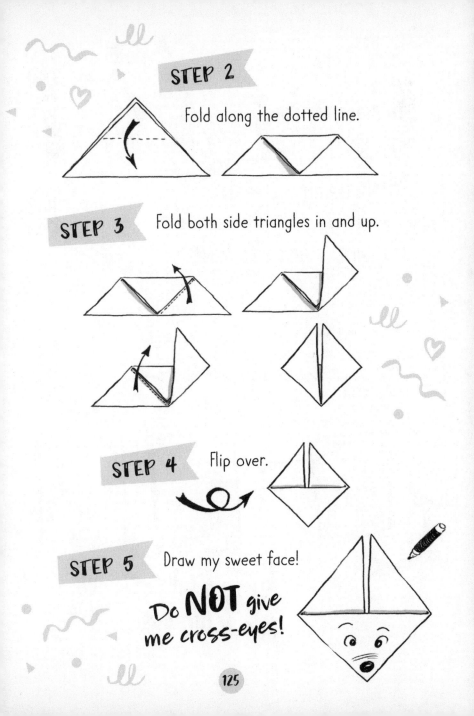

STEP 2

Fold along the dotted line.

STEP 3

Fold both side triangles in and up.

STEP 4

Flip over.

STEP 5

Draw my sweet face!

Do **NOT** give me cross-eyes!

125

TO MAKE MY BOW:

You will need a rectangle
of **coloured paper, glue**
and **scissors**. Colour in dots so that the
bow will look **JUST LIKE MINE!**

STEP 1 Fold the rectangle
in half and cut out this shape.

It is a bit
like a big eye.

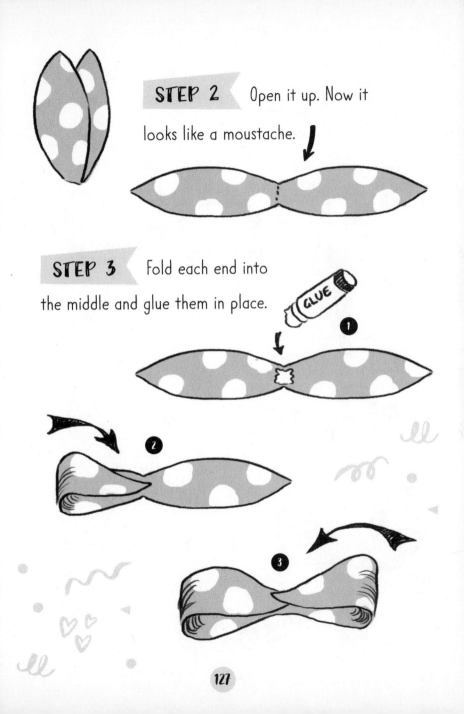

STEP 2 Open it up. Now it looks like a moustache.

STEP 3 Fold each end into the middle and glue them in place.

GLUE

STEP 4 Cut a short strip of paper.
Glue it to the back of the bow.

Loop it around the bow a few times
and glue the other end in place.

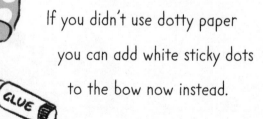

If you didn't use dotty paper
you can add white sticky dots
to the bow now instead.

Voila!
A PERFECT bow.

totally cute

Make one for your origami fox and one for you. You can even make them for your dolls.

Have you read EVERY GINGER GREEN book?

GINGER GREEN IS ABSOLUTELY MAD FOR Birthdays!

(mostly)

Ginger is turning **EIGHT** and she's having an **exceptionally royal PRINCESS PARTY**. There will be crowns, a **FANCY** castle cake AND EVEN → **SPARKLE SLIME**.

But what happens when *Crazy Maisy* and **No-Pants Penny** get out of control?

Ginger Green is all about **friendship, FUN,** and **laughter** – even in the face of ⟩⟩ **DISASTER!** ⟨⟨

Ginger is going backyard camping with her **BFF** Lottie! She's excited about having a campfire, sleeping in a tent and even a **MIDNIGHT FEAST.** But what happens when their snuggly sleepover doesn't go to plan?

THE **NOT-MUCH** Sleepover Starring **GINGER GREEN**

BY KIM KANE & JON DAVIS

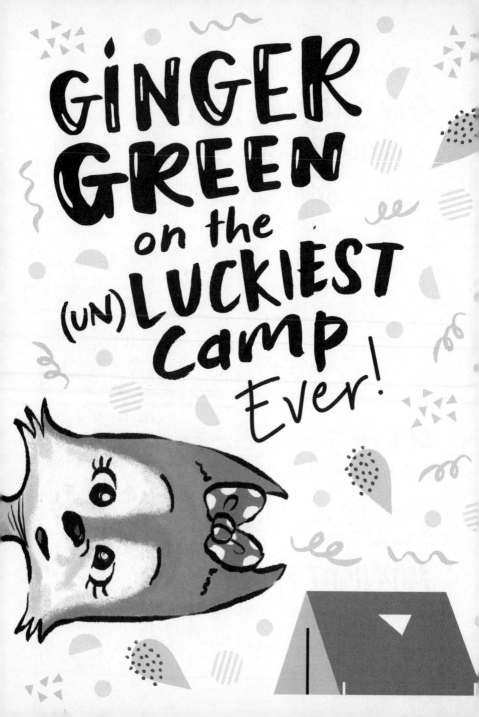

Ginger **KNOWS** that she is going to **LOVE** school camp – it's got sing-a-longs, bunk beds and ➤ **RED JELLY** ◀ **GALORE!**

But what happens when she's put in **Cabin Four**, the **UNLUCKIEST** cabin of all?

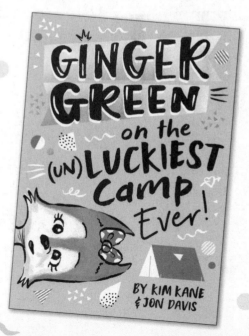

GINGER GREEN on the (UN)LUCKIEST Camp Ever!

BY KIM KANE & JON DAVIS

About the author and illustrator

KIM KANE is an award-winning Australian author who writes for children and teens. Her books include the CBCA short-listed picture book *Family Forest*, and her time-slip children's novel *When the Lyrebird Calls*. **Ginger Green** is the second series starring this funny and feisty fox. Ginger first appeared in *Ginger Green, Play Date Queen*, a beloved first-reader series.

Pirates, old elephants, witches in bloomers, bears on bikes, ugly cats, sweet kids – **JON DAVIS** does it all! Based in the Lake District, England, Jon has illustrated more than 60 kids' books for publishers across the globe, including *Ginger Green, Play Date Queen*!